the MiLO & JAZZ MYSTERIES

2

THE CASE OF THE POISONED PIG

by Lewis B. Montgomery
illustrated by Amy Wummer

The KANE PRESS
New York

Library of Congress Cataloging-in-Publication Data

Montgomery, Lewis B.
The case of the poisoned pig / by Lewis B. Montgomery ;
illustrated by Amy Wummer.
p. cm. — (The Milo & Jazz mysteries ; 2)
Summary: When Jazz's pet piglet gets sick and the veterinarian suspects it was
poisoned, she and Milo use their detective skills to try to figure out who did it.
ISBN 978-1-57565-286-3 (pbk.) — ISBN 978-1-57565-289-4 (lib. bdg.)
[1. Pigs—Fiction. 2. Pigs as pets—Fiction. 3. Pets—Fiction. 4. Mystery and
detective stories.] I. Wummer, Amy, ill. II. Title.
PZ7.M7682Cas 2009
[Fic]—dc22
2008027537

10 9 8 7 6 5 4 3 2 1

First published in the United States of America in 2009 by Kane Press, Inc.
Printed in Hong Kong.

Book Design: Edward Miller

The Milo & Jazz Mysteries is a trademark of Kane Press, Inc.

www.kanepress.com

For Cassidy's Aunt Sherry:

a new pig for your collection!—L.B.M.

CHAPTER ONE

Milo stared up at the classroom clock. How come the last few minutes of the school day always felt like hours, but recess seemed to zip by in three seconds?

A flash of purple caught his eye. He turned. It was a purple flowered clog.

The clog was on the foot of his friend Jazz. She was using it to kick a folded note across the floor between their desks.

He reached for it with his sneaker. Almost—almost—

"Milo!"

Uh-oh.

Ms. Ali, their teacher, held out her hand. "All right. Let's have that note."

Slowly he got up. Someone giggled. Ms. Ali tapped her foot as Milo walked to the front of the room.

He handed her the paper. She unfolded it. Her eyebrows scrunched. She turned it over and looked at the back, then at the front again.

"It's blank." She looked at Milo. "Why would someone pass you a blank sheet of paper?"

He shrugged. "Um . . . maybe they forgot to write a note?"

Everyone in the class was giggling now. Frowning, Ms. Ali gave him the paper, and he went back to his seat.

While Ms. Ali called for quiet, Milo pulled out his invisible–ink pen. Using an open book as a shield, he shone the pen's special light on Jazz's note.

He clicked off the light and glanced at Jazz. A surprise! Could it be a new case?

Milo and Jazz were detectives in training. They got lessons in the mail from world-famous private eye Dash Marlowe. With a little help from Dash, they solved real-life mysteries.

When the bell rang, Jazz met Milo in the hall. "Whew!" she said. "I sure am glad you gave me that invisible–ink pen."

"Me, too. So, what's the surprise?"

She smiled. "You'll see."

"Give me a hint," he said as they walked toward his brother Ethan's kindergarten room. "Where is it?"

"At my house."

"Is it Dylan?" he asked. "Did he lose something again?" Dylan was Jazz's teenage brother. Not long ago his lucky socks had disappeared, and they had tracked them down.

Jazz said, "I think he's lost his mind. Wait until you see the car he bought."

"That's the surprise?"

"No, the surprise is something *good*."

They picked Ethan up and headed home. Ethan skipped ahead, hands in his jacket pockets, singing a dinosaur song. He was crazy about dinosaurs.

"Dig, dig, dig, dig up the dinosaurs. . . ."

"How about another hint?" Milo asked Jazz.

"It starts with *P*," she said.

A surprise starting with *P*. "Party?"

"Nope."

He thought again. "Popcorn?"

"Nope."

"Pirate ship?"

Jazz gave him a look.

"Candy!" yelled Ethan.

"Huh? Candy doesn't start with *P*," Milo said.

"Look!" His brother waved a plastic Easter egg. Something rattled inside.

Candy. Mmm. "Can I have some?" Milo asked.

Quickly, Ethan shoved the egg back in his pocket. "Uh-uh. I'm saving it."

Milo rolled his eyes. He'd gobbled everything out of his own Easter basket except the plastic grass. But Ethan let himself eat just one piece a day. One single jelly bean. One little cream-filled egg. One pink or green foil-wrapped piece of chocolate. At this rate he'd have Easter candy until Halloween.

Jazz's house looked just the same as usual, at least from the outside.

"So, where's the surprise?" Milo asked as they walked up the steps.

"You'll see." She opened the door.

Zoom!

A black-and-white blur shot out. Before he knew what was happening, it dashed between his legs and hurtled off the porch. "Catch her!" Jazz yelled.

Milo ran one way. Jazz ran the other. When the animal stopped for a second, they both dove. *Bonk.*

Ouch.

Jazz rubbed her head. "Did you get her?"

"No, did you?"

"*I* got her," Ethan said.

Milo looked up at the tiny, squirming animal cradled in his brother's arms.

Was it a puppy? No.

A kitten? No.

"Holy cow," he said. "It's a pig!"

CHAPTER TWO

"This is our new pet," Jazz said. "Her name is Eugenia."

Ethan stared at the tiny pig. "Huge what?"

"Yooj-EEN-ya," Jazz repeated more slowly. "Isn't she cute?"

Milo stared too. "I thought pigs were pink."

"Not all of them," Jazz said.

Round-eyed, Ethan whispered, "She's so *little.*"

"She's just a baby. And she's a potbellied pig. They're extra-small." Jazz held out her hands, but Ethan squeezed the piglet tighter.

"Can I hold her one more minute? Please?"

"Okay, but don't squish her," Jazz said. "And don't let her go. This morning she made a mess of Mrs. Budge's prize petunias." She pointed. In the yard next door, a lady was digging up a bed of trampled flowers. She did *not* look happy.

"Your teeny little piglet did all that?" Milo asked.

Jazz nodded glumly. "Now Mom says
I have to pay Mrs. Budge back by helping
in her garden. And she's such a grouch!"

"How come you didn't tie the pig up?"

"We did, but she got loose somehow.
My dad calls her Teeny Houdini."

The door opened again, and Jazz's
older sister, Vanessa, rushed out. She
spotted the piglet.

"Queenie!" she said. "How did you get out again?"

"Queenie?" Milo glanced at Jazz. "I thought you said her name was Eugenia."

"It *is*," she said.

"Is not," Vanessa said, fists on hips.

"Is too!"

RrrrrrRRRRRRRACKACKACKACK-ackack! A loud noise from the garage drowned out the two girls. It sounded like a lawnmower choking on a weed whacker.

Their older brother Dylan strolled out wiping oily hands on his jeans.

"That car sounds even worse than it looks," Jazz said.

"Oh, yeah?" said Dylan. "See if I drive *you* anywhere." He looked down at

Ethan and the pig playing in the grass.

"Hey, Spike. Made a new friend?"

Spike?

"How many names does this pig have?" Milo asked.

Dylan laughed. "Four so far. One for each of us kids. Chris calls her Pigasus."

One piglet with four names? "Um . . . isn't that a little confusing?" Milo said.

"Dad gave us a week to decide," Jazz explained. "If we can't all agree on a name by then, he'll pick one himself."

Vanessa shuddered. "Last time he did that, we ended up with a goldfish called Glub."

"Why don't you just agree to Eugenia, then?" Jazz said.

"Why don't *you* agree to Queenie?"

"Eugenia doesn't want a silly name like Queenie," Jazz said. "Do you, Eugenia?"

Vanessa marched off in a huff.

"Want to check out my wheels?" Dylan asked Milo.

"Sure!" he said.

Jazz made a face, but she followed them to the garage.

Milo's jaw dropped. Wow.

One of the car doors hung open in a funny way. The hood was propped up with a stick, and rusty parts lay scattered on a bench. Something sticky dripped into a spreading puddle on the floor.

Dylan beamed. "Like it?"

"It's . . . it's . . ." Milo wasn't sure what
to say. "That's some car."

"It'll be even better once it's all fixed
up." Dylan gave the car a friendly pat,
and a hubcap fell off.

Milo smiled politely. Then he and Jazz
made for the door.

"See what I mean?" Jazz said. "My brother is as nutty as a bag of trail mix."

They came around the corner of the house and saw Ethan still playing with the pig.

Then Jazz stopped short. "Oh, no. It's Gordy Fletcher."

CHAPTER THREE

Gordy Fletcher was in their class at
school. He was always doing things like
sticking KISS ME signs on kids' backs.
Or asking them if they had studied for
the test when there wasn't a test that day.

Gordy was standing by his scooter.
A big white plastic thing with tubes
sticking out was slung across his back.
He was eyeing the piglet.

"What is *that*?" Gordy asked.

"It's Huge," Ethan said.

Gordy stared at the pig. "Doesn't look too huge to me."

Ethan pointed at the tubey thing on Gordy's back. "What's *that*? Is it an alien space blaster?"

Gordy smirked. "You got it." He slung it off and aimed it at the piglet. "Freeze! Or you're bacon bits." He laughed.

Jazz stormed up. "Gordy Fletcher, you leave my pig alone!"

Scowling, Gordy slung the blaster on his back again. Then, suddenly, he grinned.

"Hey, that was a great trick, passing that blank note in class today," he said. "I want to shake your hand." Gordy stuck his hand out, and Milo shook it.

BZZZZZZZZ!

Milo jumped back, yanking his hand away. Doubled over laughing, Gordy showed the buzzer hidden in his palm.

Jazz glared at him. "Why don't you pick on someone your own age? Like a two-year-old."

"Aw, come on. Can't you take a joke?" Still laughing, Gordy rode off on his scooter.

"Are you okay?" Jazz asked Milo.

He nodded. "Startled me, that's all."

"Be glad he doesn't live on your street. You know how many times he's put fake dog poop on our lawn?" She sighed.

Ethan refused to leave the piglet, so Milo called home and asked if they could stay awhile. Then he and Jazz made a snack and started on their homework.

"Let's do this in invisible ink," he said. "Then Ms. Ali can't see if it's wrong."

"And then she'll give us a zero," Jazz said.

Hmm. Good point.

Ethan tore in behind Eugenia-Queenie-Spike-Pigasus. They chased each other in circles around the kitchen table.

Suddenly the piglet stopped. A strange noise came from the back of her throat: *Eh-eh-eh*.

Jazz scooped her up. "What's wrong, Eugenia?"

Eh-eh-eh.

"I think she's choking!" Jazz said.

"Maybe we should do the Heimlich on her," said Milo.

Eh-eh-eh.

"How do you do that?"

"I'm not sure exactly. I think you hug the person hard around the waist."

"Do pigs have waists?"

Eh-eh-eh . . . blehhhh.

They stared at the puddle of pig puke.

"Well," Jazz said, "she isn't choking."

Milo groaned. "She threw up on my homework!"

Jazz set the piglet on the floor. Ethan knelt down and patted her. "Do you feel better now, Huge?"

The pig threw up again. Milo figured that meant "no."

"We'd better take her to the vet," Jazz said. "She's just a baby, after all."

"Ms. Ali is never going to believe a pig puked on my homework," Milo said.

"Maybe the vet can write you an excuse?"

Ethan insisted on coming along to the vet's office too.

"She's not our pet," Milo said.

"But I love her!"

"You just met her."

"I don't care. I love her more than Easter candy. More than Grandma Judy. More than dinosaurs." Ethan hugged the pig tightly.

"Careful," Jazz warned. "You'll make her puke again."

"He's going to make *me* puke," Milo said.

The vet's waiting room was full of animals: an orange kitten, two hamsters, a fat little puppy, and a big drooly dog. But no other pigs.

When their turn came, Dr. Soo said, "Well, now, and who is this?"

"*Eugenia.*" Jazz smiled as the vet scribbled the name on his chart.

While they told him what had happened, Dr. Soo picked up the piglet and felt her all over. He peered in her eyes and ears and down her throat. "Hmm. Mm-hmm. Looks pretty healthy."

"So why did she throw up?" Jazz asked.

Dr. Soo looked thoughtful. "I can't be sure," he said. "But it looks to me like a case of poisoning."

CHAPTER FOUR

Poisoning?

Jazz gasped. "But she's only a piglet. Who would do an awful thing like that?"

Milo pictured a gloved hand tapping a drop of sickly green liquid into a bowl of pig chow. Could this be their next case?

Dr. Soo laughed. "I wasn't suggesting foul play—that she was poisoned on purpose. I'm sure it was an accident." He picked up a leaflet and gave it to Jazz.

"A lot of ordinary household items can be dangerous for pets."

Milo read over Jazz's shoulder.

KEEPING YOUR PIG SAFE

Pigs love to explore. They also love to eat. But sometimes they eat things that aren't good for them.

Common pig poisons include:

- salt (in large amounts)
- pennies
- coffee, tea, and chocolate
- household cleaners
- soap
- sunblock
- aspirin and other pain medicines
- automobile coolant (antifreeze)
- oleander and other poisonous plants

Pig-proof your house and yard! Make sure these items are placed out of reach of your pet pig.

Antifreeze!
Milo thought of the sticky puddle under Dylan's car.  He asked Jazz, "Has Eugenia been in the garage?"

Jazz shrugged. "I don't think so. Unless she got in there while we were at school."

Dr. Soo checked his watch. "Whatever she ate, it was within the last few hours." He set the piglet on the floor. She trotted around, snuffling curiously. "At any rate, she seems fine now. If you go home and do some pig-proofing, you shouldn't have any more trouble."

When they got back, Jazz tied the pig's leash to the porch. "You stay here while we make the house safe for you." She glanced next door. Mrs. Budge was still hard at work in her torn-up garden. "And please be good."

"I'll take care of her," Ethan promised, holding her to his cheek. "Right, Huge?"

"*Eugenia*," Jazz corrected.

Ethan didn't seem to notice.

They went through the house room by room. Every time they found an item from the list, they moved it way up high where the pig couldn't reach.

Milo had just climbed up on the toilet to put the soap on a high shelf when Dylan walked in. He was covered in grease. "Whoa! I need that soap."

While Dylan scrubbed, Jazz explained about the pig-proofing and read him the list of poisons.

"Antifreeze, huh?" Dylan said.

"I saw something leaking from your car," said Milo.

"That's just water from the radiator." Dylan paused. "Well, and a little engine oil. And maybe some brake fluid. But I'll clean it up, anyway. Don't want Spike getting sick."

"Eugenia," Jazz said.

"Whatever."

They heard the front door slam.

A moment later, Ethan rushed in. "Milo! Jazz! That space alien boy is back—and he's shooting at Huge!"

CHAPTER FIVE

Gordy Fletcher stood on the sidewalk holding his blaster. The piglet dashed back and forth at the end of her leash, squealing. As they rushed toward him, Gordy took aim.

"Stop!" Milo yelled.

Gordy put his mouth up to one of the plastic tubes. His cheeks puffed out, and something small and white shot past the piglet's ear.

Jazz ran up and wrenched the weapon
out of Gordy's hands.

"Hey! Give that back!" he yelled.

"You'll get it up your nose if you shoot
at my pig again."

"But she likes it!" Gordy protested.
"Right, Bacon Bits?"

Jazz glared at him.

"She's eaten six already." Gordy

laughed. "What a pig. Get it? A pig!"

"Six *what?*" Milo asked.

"Marshmallows."

Milo stared at the white plastic tubes. "That thing shoots marshmallows?"

Gordy nodded. "I made it myself."

Wow! A homemade marshmallow shooter. Awesome.

Frowning, Jazz handed it back to

Gordy. "She shouldn't be eating all those marshmallows."

"They're only mini marshmallows."

"Well, she's a mini pig," Jazz said. "Six of those for her is like sixty for us."

Milo wondered how he'd feel if he ate sixty marshmallows. Probably not so good.

Wait a minute. . . .

"You were here before," he said to Gordy. "When you buzzed my hand."

Gordy looked nervous. "Yeah. So?"

Milo turned to Jazz. "Remember? He was in the yard when we came out of the garage. He had the shooter then, too. What if she ate some marshmallows and—"

Jazz broke in. "And then got sick!" She pointed at Gordy. "You! You did it! You poisoned Eugenia!"

"What?" Gordy backed away.

"Pig poisoner!"

"You're crazy! I didn't do anything!"
Gordy shot a marshmallow at Jazz. It fell
short. He turned and ran.

She hollered after him, "And you're a
bad shot, too!"

Milo stared at her. Was this Jazz?
Logical, calm, let's-not-jump-to-
conclusions Jazz?

"We don't *know* if Gordy gave her

marshmallows before," he pointed out. "When we came out of the garage, it looked like he had just shown up."

Jazz shook her head stubbornly. "Didn't you see how scared he looked?"

"I'd look scared, too, if someone screamed 'pig poisoner' at me," he said. "Anyway, marshmallows aren't even on the list of poisons. Maybe they're not bad for pigs."

"Of course they're bad for pigs," Jazz said. "They're bad for everybody. You know what's in them?"

"Sugar?"

"Worse than that. Vanessa told me Dylan told her they make them with ground-up hooves and bones from cows and pigs."

Pigs? "You mean—"

Jazz nodded. "Eugenia's a *cannibal*."

Yuck. No wonder she threw up. He sure wouldn't want to eat anything made from people feet.

He glanced over at the piglet. Ethan had let her off her leash, and they were chasing each other around. Mrs. Budge looked on sourly from the yard next door.

"Ethan," Milo called. "Did you see Gordy shooting marshmallows before?"

Ethan stopped and stared at him. "Sure. Then Jazz took his blaster away."

Milo shook his head. "I mean, *before*. The last time he was here."

"That *was* the last time he was here," Ethan insisted.

"No, I mean—" Oh, forget it. Little kids were hopeless.

"Maybe Mrs. Budge saw something," Jazz suggested. "You could ask her."

"You ask her. She's your neighbor."

"But she's mad at me about Eugenia."

Milo shot a glance at Mrs. Budge. She didn't look like she was in the mood to chat. Especially not about a pig. But there was no one else to ask.

He crossed the driveway.

"Excuse me—"

Mrs. Budge's head snapped up.

He gulped.

"Yes? What is it?" she said.

"Um . . . nice flowers!" he blurted out.

She looked at her wrecked flower bed, then stared at him.

"I mean—they must have been nice."

Grimly, she said, "They *were*."

Jazz came over. "Mrs. Budge, I'm really sorry about what Eugenia did. She doesn't know any better. It won't happen again." She smiled hopefully.

Mrs. Budge didn't smile back. "No," she said firmly. "It won't."

As they walked away, she mumbled something else. Milo couldn't be certain, but it sounded like, "I'm going to make good and sure of that."

CHAPTER SIX

Saturday morning Milo was polishing off
his third stack of pancakes when the mail
arrived.

"Something for you," his dad said. He
was holding out a plain brown envelope
with *DM* in the upper left-hand corner.

Dash Marlowe! A new detective
lesson! Milo tore the envelope open,

getting it sticky with syrup, and unfolded
the letter inside.

Look for a Pattern

Ever wonder why detectives are called
private eyes? Because they see things other
people don't: patterns. Find the pattern in
the clues you gather, and you'll solve your
case.

One day, the owner of the ritziest
department store in Paris called. He was
beside himself with worry. Three days
earlier, a woman had walked out of his store
carrying a suitcase. Suspicious, the guards
stopped her. After all, who brings a suitcase
to go shopping?

She must be stealing something big, they figured—a dozen pairs of designer shoes, or their entire stock of silver spoons. But when they opened the suitcase, it was empty.

The next day, the guards spotted the same woman walking out with an even bigger suitcase. They stopped her again and opened up the suitcase. Empty.

The third day, the suitcase was so big the woman could hardly carry it. This time, the guards were determined to find out what she was stealing. They examined the suitcase from top to bottom, searching for a secret hiding place, but they found nothing. Finally, they had to let her go.

That was when they sent for me, world-famous private eye, Dash Marlowe. I listened as the owner, nearly weeping, told me the whole story. Then I told him what the woman was stealing.

Suitcases.

There was more, but Milo wanted to share it with his partner. Carrying his plate to the sink, he said, "I'm going over to Jazz's, okay?"

"I want to go too!" Ethan said.

Milo sighed. "Can't you play with your own friends for once?"

"Huge *is* my friend. I love her more than Gran—"

"Okay, fine, you can come," Milo said quickly. He didn't think his mom would be too pleased to hear Ethan compare their grandma to a pig. Especially since he preferred the pig.

When they got to Jazz's house, they found Eugenia-Queenie-Spike-Pigasus tied to the front porch. She seemed pretty perky for a cannibal.

Ethan ran to her and scooped her up, cooing, "Who's the nicest piggy in the whole wide world? Do you want some kisses? Mmm?" He rubbed his nose against her little snout. Yuck.

"Milo!"

It was Jazz's voice. Milo turned, but he didn't see anyone.

An arm waved from behind a shrub in Mrs. Budge's yard. "Over here!"

CHAPTER SEVEN

Milo ran over. "How come you're hiding? Are you spying on someone?" Maybe Jazz had spotted Mrs. Budge doing something suspicious!

"I'm not hiding," Jazz said. "I'm pruning." She stood up. "Remember? I have to pay back Mrs. Budge for what Eugenia did to her garden."

He made a face. "Oh. Yeah."

"It's not so bad, actually. Mrs. Budge has been telling me all kinds of neat stuff about plants. She really knows a lot."

While Jazz worked, Milo read the new lesson from Dash Marlowe out loud. After the story about patterns, Dash wrote about how to gather evidence by talking to people who might know something about the case—suspects, witnesses, or experts:

Of course, people might not tell you the whole story. They might leave something out, not realizing it's important. They might forget. They might even lie.

Your task is to fill in the blanks—to figure out what really happened without having to be told.

Milo stopped reading. Mrs. Budge was coming toward them. She was carrying a tray of lemonade and cookies. And she was smiling!

While they ate, she inspected the shrub that Jazz had pruned. "You did a lovely job on this oleander bush, Jasmyne. You have a real green thumb."

Oleander. Why did that sound so familiar?

"I really am sorry about your flowers," Jazz told her again. "I'll keep working as long as you want me to. And I won't let Eugenia—"

"Oh, you've done enough," Mrs. Budge said. "As for your pig—well, I don't think that will be a problem very much longer." Her smile grew wider.

Milo stared at Mrs. Budge. What did she mean? He tried to catch Jazz's eye, but she was looking in a different direction.

"Oh, no. Not *him* again," Jazz said.

Gordy Fletcher stood on the sidewalk watching Ethan try to teach the piglet to roll over.

When he saw Jazz headed toward him, Gordy backed away. "I didn't touch old Bacon Bits, okay?"

"Stop calling her that!" Jazz yelled.

"Why? *You* called *me* a pig poisoner!"

Gordy had a point there.

Milo glanced at the pig, then at Jazz. "Did she get sick at all again last night? After the marshmallows?"

"No," she admitted. "But—"

"See?" Gordy said. "So take it back!"

Hands on hips, Jazz stared at him. Finally she said, "Okay. You're not the one who poisoned her . . . maybe."

For a second, Gordy looked annoyed. Then he grinned. "Good enough for me. No hard feelings." Reaching in his jacket, he pulled out a can. "I'll even let you have some of my jelly beans."

Jazz rolled her eyes. "What's inside? A snake that jumps out at you?"

"Geez! I was only trying to be nice." Gordy peeled the lid open. "See?"

Milo peeked inside. Jelly beans. Wow. Gordy really *was* just being nice!

He grabbed a handful and tossed them into his mouth.

Yecch!

Choking and sputtering, he spit them out. "What *is* that?"

Gordy was laughing too hard to answer. Finally, he wheezed, "I painted them with the bad-tasting stuff my sister puts on her nails to keep from biting them. Pretty nasty, huh?"

Just then Ethan ran up holding the piglet. "Huge is acting funny!"

Eh-eh-eh.

Milo and Jazz stared at each other in alarm. Not again!

Gordy's grin vanished. "Is she okay?"

Eh-eh-eh.

"Hey, I think she's choking." Taking the pig from Ethan, Gordy peered into her open mouth.

Milo said, "I wouldn't—"

Blehhhh.

CHAPTER EIGHT

"Look on the bright side," Milo said.
"Your pig threw up on Gordy Fletcher."

Jazz frowned. "It's not funny. How did
Eugenia get sick again? We pig-proofed
the entire house."

Milo thought. "Has she been anywhere
else this morning?"

"Outside. But she was with Ethan."

"Maybe he fed her something," Milo said. "We should talk to him."

They found his brother curled up on the living room couch with the piglet.

"Shh." Ethan put his finger to his lips. "She's sleeping."

"Ethan," Jazz said. "You didn't give Eugenia anything today, did you? Anything that isn't good for her?"

Ethan shook his head. "Just kisses."

Milo sighed. "That isn't what we mean." He wished Ethan would go back to dinosaurs. Ethan's dinosaur thing was annoying, but at least it didn't make him want to gag.

"Did you see anybody else feeding her anything?" Jazz asked.

"Uh-uh."

"Not Gordy Fletcher?"

"Uh-uh."

She looked at Milo. He shrugged.

As they went back to the kitchen, he thought about what Dr. Soo had said. What if it wasn't an accident after all? What if it *was* foul play?

"Does Eugenia have any enemies?"

Jazz looked at him. "Milo, she's a *pig*."

"What about Mrs. Budge?" he asked.

"Didn't you hear her? She said the pig wouldn't be a problem much longer. Maybe she's the one who's trying to—" He lowered his voice. "*Do her in.*"

Jazz frowned, then shook her head. "You saw how nice she was to us today. She even made us cookies."

Milo stared at her. Those cookies. Had they tasted funny? Suddenly he didn't feel so good.

"What's wrong?" Jazz said. "You look like Glub the time his goldfish bowl tipped over."

"My stomach hurts . . . the cookies . . ."

"Next time don't eat

so many. I feel fine." She went on, "How about Gordy?"

"Ethan said Gordy didn't give her anything."

Jazz raised an eyebrow. "He said he didn't *see* Gordy give her anything. That's different."

Milo thought about it. Gordy was . . . well, he was Gordy. But he wouldn't poison a pet pig. Would he?

"Those jelly beans!" Jazz said.

"They just tasted horrible. The nail stuff isn't poisonous," Milo told her.

"That doesn't mean it's okay for Eugenia. There were things on that list of pig poisons that were fine for people."

Milo got out his detective notebook.

He wrote:

Suspects
Gordy
Mrs. Budge

Milo looked at the list. Gordy, Mrs. Budge . . . Something was bugging him. Something Mrs. Budge had said—

"Oleander!" he exclaimed.

"What?"

"Mrs. Budge has oleander in her yard. And it was on the list of poisons!"

Jazz's eyes widened. "You mean, Eugenia might have eaten some leaves?" She frowned. "But she only got into Mrs. Budge's yard once. So the second time she got sick, she couldn't have been eating oleander."

"Unless Mrs. Budge *fed* it to her."

Jazz frowned again. "Mrs. Budge might be a little grouchy sometimes. But a pig poisoner?" She shook her head. "I say it was Gordy and the jelly beans."

"Well, I say it was Mrs. Budge."

They stared at each other.

Jazz sighed. "If only we'd caught him in the act."

"Or her," Milo added.

He tried to think. What would Dash do? Slowly, he said, "Maybe it's not too late."

"What do you mean?"

"It's happened twice. It could happen again." He smiled. "But this time, we'll be ready."

CHAPTER NINE

Hippety, hoppety. Hippety, hoppety.

Behind the bushes, a chocolate bunny hopped onto Milo's knee. He made a grab for it, but it hopped away.

"Come on, Ethan," he whispered. "Let me have a bite of that bunny. I'm starving."

Hippety. "I can't. I'm saving it."

"One ear? The tail?"

Hoppety. Ethan shook his head.

Milo pulled his notebook from his pocket. *Rule #1 for stakeouts*, he wrote. *BRING A SNACK!*

Jazz peeked out at the piglet, who was tied to the front porch. "I'm still not so sure this is a good idea, using Eugenia as bait."

"Nothing will happen to her," Milo promised. "We've been right here watching the whole time."

And watching. And watching.

Somewhere nearby, a door slammed. A minute later, Mrs. Budge came up the front walk.

At last!

She was carrying a paper bag with leaves sticking out the top. Milo sucked in his breath. Could it be . . . oleander?

All he could see now were her legs.

Suddenly the piglet dashed forward. Mrs. Budge shrieked. The bag dropped to the ground.

The piglet happily dove at the leaves. Jazz gasped.

Then, before they could move from their hiding spot, a hand reached down and snatched the bag away.

"No, no," said Mrs. Budge. "That's not for you. You may be a pest, but I don't want you getting sick."

Rap-rap-rap. Mrs. Budge was knocking on Jazz's front door.

A second later it opened.

"I brought you some mint from my garden," Mrs. Budge said.

"Oh, thank you!" said Jazz's mom. "I love mint in my iced tea. Come on inside."

The door clicked shut.

"I *knew* it wasn't her," Jazz whispered.

They settled in to wait some more. The minutes dragged. Milo's stomach growled. He stared at Ethan's chocolate bunny until Ethan got nervous and stuffed it in his shirt.

Maybe Jazz was right. Maybe this stakeout wasn't such a good idea.

Then Gordy came down the street.

When he got to Jazz's house, he
stopped and glanced around nervously.
Then he dashed up the walk, squatted
down, and reached toward Eugenia.

"What's he doing?" Jazz hissed.

Milo peered out. "He's . . . petting her."

Then Gordy spoke.

"Who's a widdle Bacon Bits?" he said.
"Who's an itsy-bitsy piggy wiggy?"

Milo and Jazz stared at each other. *Gordy?* Talking baby talk to a pig?

Milo bit his cheek and clamped his hand over his mouth. He looked away from Jazz, who was doing the same thing. But it was no use. Their eyes met, and they exploded in laughter.

As the two detectives fell out of the bushes, Gordy jumped to his feet. His face brick red, he turned and ran.

"Itsy bitsy!" Milo choked out.

Jazz gasped, "Widdle piggy wiggy!"

When they finally stopped laughing, Milo's stomach started growling again. They left Ethan and the piglet on the porch and went in for a snack.

While Jazz raided the refrigerator,

Milo opened his notebook and stared at their short list of suspects.

Gordy. Mrs. Budge.

Jazz glanced over his shoulder. "We know it wasn't Mrs. Budge. We heard her say right out that she didn't want Eugenia getting sick."

"And it couldn't have been Gordy, either," said Milo. "He'd never let widdle Bacon Bitsy eat anything icky."

He crossed off Gordy. He crossed off Mrs. Budge.

Suspects
~~Gordy~~
~~Mrs. Budge~~

"So much for our list," Milo said.

"Maybe we're looking at this wrong," said Jazz.

"What do you mean?"

"Well, Dash said to *look for a pattern*. That means something that's the same each time. Maybe what we need to do is write down everything we know about the two times Eugenia was poisoned."

She grabbed the notebook and wrote:

First time
_____

where: kitchen
when: BPP

Second time
_____

where: yard
when: APP

"What's BPP and APP?" Milo asked.

"Before pig-proofing and after pig-proofing, of course." Jazz tapped the pen. "What else?"

He shrugged. "The puke looked pretty much the same both times. Kind of brown and—"

"Got it. Thanks." Jazz made a face. "How about people? Gordy was around, and Mrs. Budge—"

"And us."

"It wasn't Gordy, and it wasn't Mrs. Budge. And it sure wasn't us. Now what? No one else was there both times . . . except for Ethan."

Milo looked at Jazz.

Jazz looked at Milo.

"*Ethan!*" they yelled.

When he came inside, Jazz asked, "Ethan, are you *sure* you didn't give Eugenia anything bad to eat?"

He shook his head.

"Nothing at all?"

"I *told* you. I just gave her kisses. Huge loves kisses."

Milo rolled his eyes. "Ethan—"

"But they're all gone now," his brother went on. "That's why I brung the bunny. I bet she loves bunnies, too."

Wait a minute.

Bunnies. Kisses.

And a poisoned pig.

"Ethan . . . do you mean . . . *chocolate* kisses?"

Ethan nodded happily. Then he reached in his pocket and dug out a big handful of crumpled pink and green foil wrappers.

"From my Easter basket. I let Huge have *all* my kisses. They're her favorite."

"He didn't mean to hurt her. He just wanted to give her the nicest thing he had, and that was chocolate. He loves that pig."

Jazz smiled. "I know. But if we hadn't caught him in time, he might have loved her to *death!*"

"You know what *I* can't believe?"

"What?" Jazz said.

"Ethan gave Eugenia a ton of Easter candy, and he wouldn't give me any—not one tiny bite. Me, his own brother."

Jazz laughed. Then she said, "By the way . . . her name isn't Eugenia."

"It's not? How come? Did 'Queenie' win?"

"Yuck! No!"

"Spike? Pigasus?"

She shook her head. "We picked a new name. Actually, it was Gordy's idea."

"Not Bacon Bits!"

"Not exactly." Jazz waved an arm at the pig. "May I present . . . Bitsy."

"Bitsy," Milo said. "That's a pretty good name for a mini pig. Though she can sure cause mega trouble!"

"Well, the trouble is all over," Jazz said. "Ethan won't give her chocolate anymore. And we don't have to worry about her getting into Mrs. Budge's garden."

Milo looked at the new fence guarding the freshly replanted flower bed. "I feel so silly for suspecting Mrs. Budge," he said. "All her talk of taking care of the pig problem. And she just meant putting up a fence!"

Jazz said, "Yeah, but you—"

Her next words were drowned out by a roar. A moment later, Dylan's car nosed slowly down the driveway.

Grinning, he leaned out the open window. "Hey, kids. Want a ride?"

"Wow! You got it running!" Milo said.

"Don't look so shocked." He patted the side. "This baby's going places."

As the car eased forward, Bitsy the piglet dashed across the lawn toward the driveway.

"Dylan!" Jazz yelled. "Watch out!"

Startled, Dylan swung the steering wheel. The car veered away from Bitsy—and into the new fence. The car stopped with its two front tires planted smack in Mrs. Budge's flower bed.

Milo and Jazz stared.

"Um . . . what was that you said about the trouble being over?" Milo asked.

Jazz shook her head slowly. Then she said, "You know how Dash says to look for a pattern?"

"Yeah?"

"I think I see one now."

Milo said, "You mean about how Mrs. Budge's flowers keep getting smushed?"

"No," Jazz said. "I mean about how two things always seem to go together. Trouble . . . and us!"

SUPER SLEUTHING STRATEGIES

By the time Dash wrote back to Milo and Jazz, Mrs. Budge had replanted her flowers. This time she planted them on the other side of her yard.

Greetings, Milo and Jazz,

Congratulations on solving your second case! I know what you mean about snacks and stakeouts. I too learned that lesson the hard way— when I waited nine hours under the table at Ray's Ribs to catch the BBQ Bandit. While you're waiting for your next case, you can chew on these mini-mysteries and puzzles. Food for thought!

Happy Sleuthing!
—Dash Marlowe

Warm Up!

Warm up and stretch those brain muscles. . . .
If you remember the last batch of Brain Stretchers, you'll know where the puzzles are. And if you don't remember? Then puzzle it out!

1. What starts with an E, ends with an E, and usually contains only one letter?
2. How much dirt is in a hole 2 feet deep and 2 feet wide?
3. Why are 1990 dollar bills worth more than 1989 dollar bills?

Spot the Clue!

The more you train your eyes the better observer you'll be. Some cases give your eyes a real workout—like the Case of the Twin Tattoos.

I'm never happy when a crime involves twins. This time, for instance, I knew identical twin Matt was the smuggler. But each twin insisted that he was Will, not Matt.

How did I know which brother was which? Even their tattoos were identical—*almost!* Can you spot which tattoo belonged to Matt and which belonged to Will?

Doing Time: A Logic Puzzle

Cell 1   Cell 5   Cell 9

Three thieves are in the same prison. Can you work out what book each one is reading and which cell each belongs in?

Look at the clues and fill in the answer box where you can. Then read the clues again to find the answer.

1. Rocky is in Cell 1 but isn't reading *Famous Prisons*.
2. Sal is reading *Famous Prisoners*.
3. Louie isn't in Cell 5.
4. One of the prisoners is reading *Famous Prison Breaks*.

Answer Box

	Cell 1	Cell 5	Cell 9
Name			
Book			

Poison Picnic: A Mini-Mystery

I always enjoy a good poisoning case—like this tough and tricky one.

It was a boiling hot day in August. Melanie was the first guest to arrive at Miss Hattie's annual picnic. She was so thirsty, she immediately had a glass of lemonade with ice. But she was still melting in the sun so she left early.

That evening she found out that the lemonade had been poisoned! Twenty-one people had all gotten very, very sick—everyone but Melanie.

Why was Melanie the only one who was perfectly fine? Some people thought they knew the answer—Melanie was the poisoner! But that wasn't it.

So how did everyone but Melanie get poisoned? (Hint: The culprit had carried out the poisonous plot just before the picnic started.)

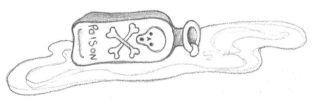

Answer: The poison was in the ice cubes! They were frozen solid when Melanie drank her lemonade. But after she left, the August sun quickly melted them and the poison seeped into the lemonade. By the way, I eventually did figure out who the poisoner was—Miss Hattie. She'd just pretended to be sick. Turned out she was tired of hosting the annual picnic.

Pattern Puzzles

Once you find a pattern, you're a step ahead. Not only do you know what's going on, but you can even tell what may be coming!

What's next in these patterns?

1.

(Hint: Find a mirror.)

2.

Answer 1: The number 8 is in mirror writing. (The pattern is to add two to each mirror-written number: 0, 2, 4, 6, 8.)

Answer 2: A solid-line circle with a dotted-line circle inside it. There are really two parts to this pattern. First, the shapes repeat: circle, triangle, square. Second, the dotted lines go from the inside shape and then to the outside shape and so on. The best detectives can work on two things at once!

Answers for Brain Stretchers:
1. An envelope.
2. No dirt at all. A hole is empty.
3. 1990 dollars are worth one dollar more than 1989 dollars!

Don't miss Milo and Jazz's first case:

The Case of the Stinky Socks

Milo and Jazz team up to solve their very first mystery! The Wildcats' star pitcher is missing his lucky socks, and his pitching is going to pieces. But who would have stolen a pair of stinky socks? The jealous team mascot? The super-smug tennis champ? A player from the rival team? Milo and Jazz have to find the thief—and the socks—before the big game!

COMING SOON

More mysteries from your favorite detectives (in training)!
Book 3: The Case of the *Haunted* Haunted House
Book 4: The Case of the Amazing Zelda

ABOUT THE AUTHOR

Lewis B. Montgomery is the pen name of a writer whose favorite authors include CSL, EBW, and LMM. Those initials are a clue—but there's another clue, too. Can you figure out their names?

Besides writing the Milo & Jazz mysteries, LBM enjoys eating spicy Thai noodles and blueberry ice cream, riding a bike, and reading. Not all at the same time, of course. At least, not anymore. But that's another story. . . .

ABOUT THE ILLUSTRATOR

Amy Wummer has illustrated more than 50 children's books. She uses pencils, watercolors, and ink—but not the invisible kind.

Amy and her husband, who is also an artist, live in Pennsylvania . . . in a mysterious old house which has a secret hidden room in the basement!

CHAPTER TEN

Milo sat on the porch steps watching Ethan and the piglet chase each other around the front yard. Jazz was copying out their letter to Dash Marlowe in invisible ink on a purple pad. They'd told him all about how they had solved the Case of the Poisoned Pig.

"I still can't believe your little brother was the poisoner," she said.